Frank's Quantum Adventure

by PJ McFarlane

Produced by:

FriesenPress
Suite 300 – 852 Fort Street
Victoria, BC, Canada V8W 1H8

www.friesenpress.com

Distributed to the trade by The Ingram Book Company

Dedicated to my supportive family and Joe Lemmo
You were the inspiration that made this book a reality.

Foreword

It's a special honor to be asked to write a foreword for a book. And when it's for a former student, it becomes even more special. I have been teaching for thirteen years and have taught over fifteen hundred students. I've probably read in the neighborhood of over ten thousand writing samples. I've read journals, stories, essays, and even notes passed illegally from student to student. I can comfortably say that P.J. McFarlane is one of the most talented writers I've ever taught.

It didn't take long for me to identify his tremendous ability to write. I immediately noticed something different about his writing the year he was in my seventh grade class. His writing seemed "classic" and well beyond his years. The best part of his work though was how modest he was. He never bragged when he received high marks for his work, and he was always humbly willing to let me share what he had written. Yes, I was quite proud to be his teacher that year.

This entertaining story you are about to read originated as a short play that P.J. prepared for a contest. And because his play had so much success, I urged P.J. to make it into a full story. Luckily, P.J. accepted the challenge, and the story was born. He worked on it for the rest of his seventh grade year, throughout the summer, and continued in eighth grade. He kept me updated from time to time, and I read what he was working on to my current seventh graders. I knew he had something special because they couldn't get enough of what I shared! They kept asking me if he had written anymore, and were disappointed when the answer was no.

I hope you enjoy reading this story as much as I have enjoyed being a part of it. If you are ever lucky enough to actually meet P.J. you will surely see why I consider him to be a genuine "rock star".

Sincerely,

Joseph W. Lemmo

Chapter One

The Drudgery

A perfect world. What is a perfect world? When we think of a perfect world, we usually picture absolute peace. No wars, stress, or unhappiness. A world where everything goes right.

But in this world, we're far from perfect. And even though we make the best of the world we're stuck with, we all go through a period of time in which nothing goes right and it seems as though the world hates us.

Unfortunately for Frank, this sad period of time has been going on for his entire life.

Meet Frank. Frank lived a life overwhelmed by stress, confusion, and desperation. A life so mind numbingly boring and uninteresting that he sometimes wanted to rip his hair out strand by strand. Know the feeling?

He longed for excitement... an adventure is just what he needed.

Our story begins on the worst day of the week: Monday. Frank's weeklong experience of misery had begun once again. The annoying beeps emitting from his alarm clock were ringing in his eardrums. Sleepily, but forcefully, he slammed his fist on the snooze bar. But after a while, he forced himself to wake up and get ready for work.

Carefully navigating through his bedroom filled with dirty clothes scattered about, he proceeded to his small, standard, boring bathroom. It was nothing much, really. Just a toilet, a sink, and a shower. But it was enough.

As Frank gazed into the crooked mirror hanging above the sink, he realized he had a five o' clock shadow at seven in the morning. There was no time to shave, however, because he was already late.

He brushed his teeth as he sped down the stairs, almost tripping over his dog, Captain Wafers, who held up his chew toy, wagging his tail, obviously wanting to play.

"Not now, boy. I'm late," Frank said firmly to the shaggy Yorkie and walked on by. The dog whimpered and went back to sleep.

Frank then headed outside to his driveway, where his 1976 station wagon was parked. The thing was probably only worth about five hundred dollars and was gradually falling apart. He would eventually have to fix the hunk of junk. But that was just another task on his long list of stresses.

He tugged on the handle of his brown, rusted car door. It didn't budge. *That's weird...* Frank thought to himself. He knew the car was cheap and rusty, but the door had always opened. As he looked through the window of the car, he discovered the problem.

There, sitting in the keyhole, were his keys. Frank's eyes widened in disbelief. He had locked his keys inside the car! How could he have been so dumb? And on top of that, he left a melting ice cream cone in the cup holder. Could his morning get any worse? Frank sighed. There was only one thing he could do. He marched into the garage and pulled out his golf clubs. He pulled out a nine iron, raised it high into the air, and then...

WHAM! He drove the golf club into his window. Each crack gave birth to a hundred more. All the neighbors were looking at him now. This quirky young man, driving a golf club through his car window. Frank wasn't finished. But, with one more hit, the window would be obliterated.

"Fore!" Frank yelled as he violently slammed his golf club into the car window once more, this time completely shattering it. He reached through the hole where his window once was, unlocked and opened the door, and crawled in, over the tiny pieces of broken glass.

After buckling his seatbelt, he started the engine, which coughed out a puff of black smog as he backed out of the driveway. He drove out of the street and into the Parkway, hoping his day couldn't get any more frustrating.

He was changing the radio stations rapidly, looking for something that wasn't some new age bubble-pop garbage. But nothing came up. So, he checked himself in the rearview mirror. His dark black, wavy hair looked pretty clean despite the fact he had no time to take a shower this morning. But then he noticed something else in his rearview mirror... It was a cop car.

Oh, great... Frank thought to himself. *What does he want?* He wasn't speeding. His blinker wasn't on. So what *did* this mysterious cop want? Just then...

BOOM! Frank swerved out of control. Were those gunshots? Was the cop *shooting* at him? BOOM! Another gunshot! Frank's speed was rapidly decreasing until he came to a complete stop in the middle of the Parkway. Frank, still startled out of his mind, stepped out of the car to find that the cop had shot out his back two tires. The cop car had pulled over as well, and the cop stepped out of the car.

"Well, well, well... Look what we have here," the cop said as he walked towards Frank. Frank immediately knew who it was. It was Duncan. Duncan hated Frank, and was always pulling him over and giving him tickets for stupid, irrelevant reasons. Frank didn't know why Duncan disliked him so much.

"I'm going to have to give you a fine of eighty dollars," Duncan said to Frank as he munched on a chocolate doughnut with sprinkles that he always seemed to have in his hand.

"What?! Why?" Frank shouted.

"Your tires. They appear to be deflated. That is a safety hazard," said Duncan, taking another bite of his donut. He scribbled the fine in a notepad, tore it out, and handed it to Frank.

"There deflated because *you* shot them!" Frank snapped back at Duncan.

"Back sassing a cop, eh? That's another eighty dollars," Duncan replied. He scribbled another fine into his notepad and gave it to Frank.

"You're insane if you think I'm paying this! What kind of cop are you?!" yelled Frank right into Duncan's face. Frank shot Duncan a dirty look.

"Refusing to pay a fine given by a police officer, are we?" Duncan asked Frank. "That'll be..." Frank cut him off.

"Let me guess," he said, rolling his eyes. "*Another* fine?"

"Exactly!" Duncan replied, grinning. "Have a nice day." He got back into his car, gnawing on his donut, and sped down the Parkway, leaving Frank stranded with a car that wasn't drivable.

And so, Frank was forced to walk all the way to his office building. What would have been a forty-five minute drive was now at least a five hour walk. There were no taxis or buses in his little gloomy suburban neighborhood, only adding to his dismay. He wanted to just go back home. It was probably the most logical solution to his problems. But, alas, he had no sick days or personal days remaining, and missing work today would most likely get him fired. He sighed, grabbed some cough drops out of his glove box, and began walking, leaving his station wagon on the side of the road.

What would he tell his boss? Showing up to work over six hours late would surely be an outrage. He would just have to face the music. He's been in sticky situations with his employer. This was nothing he couldn't handle. Plus, showing up incredibly late was better than not showing up at all.

But, as he walked he noticed a pink bird flying above his head.

"Shoo!" he shouted at the bird, waving his arms frantically. Then the bird disappeared. People were stopping and staring at Frank, just like they had earlier this morning when he smashed his car window. Was he hallucinating? Was the bird really there? His doctor had told him about hallucinations that are caused by stress. Perhaps it was one of those.

He kept walking, and eventually he wound up at work at around 2:30. Frank worked at Figgins Incorporated, a company that manufactured and distributed paper clips, and Frank's job was to file paperwork and occasionally fix the copy machine after some idiot would try to photocopy his butt, and end up breaking the copier with his weight. There was only an hour and a half left in the workday, but at least he showed up.

As Frank walked into his building, he was greeted by Susan, the lady who worked at the front desk in the lobby.

"Frank! What a pleasure to see you!" She exclaimed quite loudly, looking up from her clunky, outdated computer. Susan had a loud, obnoxious voice, and wore too much makeup every day, but she was friendly, nonetheless. "Yikes… you're a little late it seems," she said, smiling.

"Good morning, Susan," Frank replied as he approached the front desk.

"It's the afternoon," she corrected Frank, reminding him of hit tardiness. She was still smiling as she handed Frank his time card.

"Oh, yes, of course," Frank said to Susan. He had forgotten that he was over six hours late, and was so used to saying good morning rather than good afternoon.

"You have a good day, now," Susan exclaimed, beaming.

"I'll try…" Frank muttered under his breath as he walked away. He approached the time slot and punched in.

"*You are: 6 hours and 37 minutes late*," the machine read. Frank didn't care. It wasn't his fault, after all.

He stepped into the only working elevator in the entire building (the others were either broken or under construction), which as usual, smelled like new carpet and Lysol™, alongside some kid who looked like he was about ten or eleven years old. The kid had blond, spiked up hair, a blue t-shirt, and a pair of cargo pants with about ten different pockets. Frank then pushed the small button that had the number 40 on it. He felt important working on the very top floor of his entire office. That is until the little kid quickly pushed every single button in the elevator. Frank now had a one way ticket to every single floor in the entire building. With his mouth wide open in disbelief, Frank looked at the little punk, giving him the evil eye. The boy just giggled and hopped out of the elevator once it reached the second floor.

Frank sighed and began his journey to the top floor. Why was there even a kid in his building? Frank had never seen the kid, or any kid for that matter, ever in his office. He didn't know. As he cursed the kid out in his mind, various people got in and out of the elevator. One guy even farted, filling the elevator with a noxious gas cloud that Frank couldn't escape. It was horrible. He finally reached the fortieth floor about ten minutes later, and the elevator door slowly opened.

Now all he had to do was face Mr. Figgins, his unfair, terrible boss.

Mr. Figgins was a very strange man. First of all, he was incredibly short. So short, you would probably think he was a little kid if it weren't for his old, ugly face. Every day he would show up to work wearing an eye patch, claiming he lost his eye in a "terrible lobster incident" that he never seemed to want to talk about. He insisted everyone call him Sir Figgins the Magnificent. But on top of it all, his first name was Nancy. And, yes, I'm not kidding.

Just thinking about Mr. Figgins made Frank shiver. He wondered if he could somehow sneak by his boss without him noticing. Frank could hear Mr. Figgins hollering at someone about fifteen cubicles away. Now was his chance.

He tiptoed by, past the vending machine, past the fake rubber plant, all the way to his small, cramped cubicle in the corner. Just when he thought he was home free, he heard…

"Frank!" He couldn't forget that voice. The terrible, growling voice of none other than Mr. Figgins. He marched towards Frank, his face as red as a cherry.

"Tell me, Nichols, just why are you over six hours late?" Figgins yelled, steaming with rage.

Frank wanted to tell his unruly boss that an idiot "police officer" shot out his tires, forcing him to resort to walking to work, and that a punk kid pushed all of the elevator buttons and gave him motion sickness. But Mr. Figgins didn't like excuses, so all Frank said was:

"My last name isn't Nichols. It's Smith." Then, without warning, Mr. Figgins kicked Frank in the shin. "Ow!" He cried out, writhing in pain. For a small man, Figgins sure could kick hard, and he surely didn't like being corrected.

"Don't back sass me, Nichols!" He shouted. "I'll call you whatever I please! Is that understood?"

"Yes, Mr. Figgins," Frank sighed.

"That's Sir Figgins the Magnificent to you, Nichols!" Mr. Figgins screamed, kicking Frank in the shin once more.

All Frank could say was: "Ow!" as his boss stomped off.

As he sluggishly walked into his cubicle, he noticed an incredibly huge stack of papers with a post it note that read:

Make sure it's all completed by tomorrow morning! —NF

Frank couldn't believe his eyes. There had to be at least a thousand individual pages to be completed. There was simply no way in this world he could get them all done by tomorrow. But what could he do? He had to try. It was his only logical option, his alternative being getting fired. Frank began as quickly as possible. His perseverance hadn't failed him quite yet.

But by the end of the day, he had hardly begun the monstrous task. The only thing he could do now was to spend all night filling out the thousands of papers he was assigned, which was certainly not his ideal evening.

Frank hopped onto the elevator and proceeded down to the lobby of his office building. Luckily there were no obnoxious little kids to add on to Frank's misery.

He decided to call a cab, considering he currently had a lack of a vehicle for the time being. It was five thirty, so naturally, everyone was trying to get home, and cabs were tough to find, and you'd occasionally get the one that smells like vomit, which wasn't very pleasant.

Frank hopped into a fairly good cab. The driver was nice and there didn't seem to be an aroma of puke, so that was surely a good sign. But then, an old man stepped into the cab alongside Frank, and judging by the pointy purple hat and matching robe plus the long white beard, he sort of looked like a wizard.

Things went smoothly at first, until the mysterious wizard started talking…

"Frank… Smith…" he said with a creepy tone in his voice. Frank immediately looked up. He had never seen this wizard dude in his life. So, how did he know his name?

"Do I know you from somewhere?" Frank asked the wizard, who was still staring at him.

"I sense a… disturbance," the strange wizard said, ignoring Frank's previous question.

"A disturbance? What are you going on about old man?" Frank remarked back at the wizard, who seemed to be having a flashback of some sort. There was a long awkward silence. Finally the wizard spoke once more…

"Indeed. Take this," he said, holding out his hand. There, in his palm, was a small, irregularly shaped rock. Frank took it, unsure of what he was supposed to do with it.

"Who are you? And why are you giving me this rock?" Frank snapped back. He was getting confused and frustrated. There was another long awkward silence until the wizard replied.

"Use it," he whispered at last. Frank didn't hear him.

"What?" he asked the wizard.

"USE THE ROCK TO DEFEAT THE ANTAGONIST, FRANK SMITH!" The wizard was shouting now, which startled both Frank and the cab driver.

"Inside voices, old timer!" the driver snapped back.

"Farewell, mortals!" the wizard hollered just before he dropped a smoke pellet and disappeared. The smoke filled the cab, which distracted the driver, who almost swerved off of the road.

"Who *was* that guy?" the driver asked Frank, who was just as confused as he was.

"I have no idea," Frank replied. He looked at the rock that was in his hand. What did it mean? How was he supposed to use this? It was just an ordinary rock. What tickled Frank's mind even more was the fact that he had never in his life seen or heard of this mysterious wizard before. And now he was giving him a rock, and telling him he needed to defeat the antagonist with it, whoever that was. Frank wasn't sure. So he simply pocketed the rock and tried to forget what just happened.

The driver dropped off Frank about two blocks from the isolated suburban neighborhood in which he lived. As he walked through the parkway, he noticed his car wasn't where he'd left it, meaning it had probably been towed. Frank buried his head into his hand. His entire day had been a complete nightmare. And he still had to complete the mountain of papers for Mr. Figgins', which would no doubt take all night. He'd just have to pick up his car at the impound lot tomorrow.

As Frank approached his small, run-down house, he noticed that same pink bird that was flying around his head earlier was now sitting on top of his house. Frank just stared at the bird, and the bird did the same. Maybe the bird wasn't just a hallucination. Perhaps this odd, pink dove was trying to tell him something. Whatever it was, it would have to wait. Frank was too tired to think about anything right now.

He ignored the bird and walked into his house, where he was greeted by Captain Wafers. The small dog followed Frank upstairs and into his bedroom.

Frank sat on the bed, opened his briefcase and began working on the paperwork he was assigned. He could hardly concentrate, though. Thoughts flooded his mind, primarily about the mysterious rock. What did it mean? He set the rock on his side table as Captain Wafers hopped on the bed and settled comfortably beneath Frank's feet.

He tried to focus, but it was no use. He was too distracted and tired to be productive. All he could do now was to try to forget how lousy his day was and go to sleep. So, that's exactly what he did.

Chapter Two

The Disappearance

They say Tuesday is the most productive workday. The day a lot of things get done. Not for Frank. Frank generally awoke every morning dreading about what is to come throughout the day. This particular morning, Frank awoke from his slumber to a mountain of papers, scattered about. Not exactly the ideal image to start your day. He had hardly put a dent in the ridiculous amount of work Mr. Figgins had given him.

But, Frank woke up on Tuesday morning to a different feeling. He didn't feel tired at all, in contrast to his usual fatigue-ridden mornings. He felt refreshed and ready to tackle the day, which was very unusual. Come to think of it, his alarm clock didn't wake him up. He could've sworn he set it to seven o' clock sharp, just like he did every morning.

What was even odder was that Frank's alarm clock wasn't there at all. It was almost as if it had disappeared.

He checked behind his nightstand, thinking it might have somehow become unplugged and fallen down there in the middle of the night. But it wasn't there.

Maybe someone broke in and stole it. But who would break into someone else's house to steal an alarm clock? Frank was surely confused. He checked his watch, and was shocked to see the time.

It was almost one o' clock.

Frank gasped. He had overslept, and was going to be several hours late for work for the second day in a row. As he scrambled around, desperately trying to get ready for work, he thought of something... Why should he even go to work today? After all, his car had been towed, and he had no intention of walking to work again. Plus, he hadn't completed the paperwork Mr. Figgins gave him yesterday. Whether he did or didn't show up today, he was probably going to get fired.

As Frank stood up and stretched, he came up with a fantastic realization: He had the day off.

It was just what he needed. A break from all the agony and stress that was his life. Perhaps his clock disappeared for a reason. Frank smiled a little, despite the fact that he was most likely going to lose his job. Captain Wafers bolted up the stairs, wagging his tail. He seemed pretty happy too.

Frank began to wonder how he was going to spend his day. Of course, the first thing he had to do was pick up his car at the impound lot. That was quite essential. But before that, he needed to put on pants. Those were also essential.

He stared down at Captain Wafers, who was shaking and whimpering, clearly needing to do his business.

"In a minute, boy. Hold your horses," Frank said to the impatient canine.

He pulled out a pair of ratty, slightly torn jeans from his wardrobe and put them on the ironing board. After plugging the iron into the wall socket, he started ironing his pants. But then something incredibly strange happened…

VWOOSH! In the blink of an eye, the ironing board literally vanished into thin air, inexplicably. Startled, Frank dropped the iron, which landed on his bare foot.

"YOW!" He hollered, startling Captain Wafers, who was standing beside him. Frank stood there, wondering what happened. He waved his arms where the ironing board was just a moment ago, making sure he wasn't hallucinating.

Confused, he started to think again. What had happened? Why did his ironing board vanish? Where did it go? Frank skeptically walked downstairs into his living room as Captain Wafers followed. Frank decided not to think about the ironing board too much. He was so confused about it he hadn't noticed how much his foot was in pain.

But then, as he took Neosporin™ out of his medicine cabinet along with some bandages…

VWOOSH! It happened again! The Neosporin™ bottle disappeared just like the ironing board did just a minute ago. Gone. Into thin air.

"What is happening?!" Frank shouted out loud. As he looked around his living room, he noticed there were a few things missing. The lamp. The coffee table. A few chairs. His microwave. They had probably disappeared too. At that moment, all of his thoughts turned to the rock he had received from the wizard the previous day. Was that the cause of everything vanishing? Frank wasn't sure, but he didn't want to take any chances.

And so, he marched upstairs, grabbed the rock from his nightstand, and opened the window and, without a moment of hesitation, Frank chucked the rock deep into the woods that spread throughout his surprisingly large backyard. *That was easy enough…* Frank thought to himself. He certainly wasn't about to let that stupid rock ruin his entire day off.

But when he turned around, it was there. Sitting on his counter was the rock, untouched.

"No way," Frank said. This couldn't be happening. He couldn't get rid of it. Frank was beginning to get suspicious. Something was fishy. Things aren't typically supposed to just disappear in to the air without warning. *Someone must be behind this.* Frank thought. And he wanted to get to the bottom of whatever was going on.

But how? He was confused and felt powerless. The rock, it seemed, was the source of the vanishing, and he couldn't escape its presence.

But then he got an idea. Frank's close friend, Rick just so happened to be a quantum physicist. Recently, Rick had become extremely interested in time travel and teleportation. If there was a scientific explanation for what was going on, Rick knew the answer.

VWOOSH! Frank heard something else vanish, but didn't know what it was. Then, all of a sudden, he felt a draft. *Uh, oh…* Frank thought, looking down. Sure enough, his pants were gone, revealing his polka-dotted boxers. He sprinted upstairs to get another pair, but of course, his dresser had disappeared, too. *Perfect. Just perfect.* He thought.

Frank headed downstairs and into his garage, where he pulled out his bicycle. Despite his sudden lack of pants, he still wanted to talk to Rick at his warehouse/laboratory, which was quite far away.

And so, Frank pedaled into the street. He was determined to find the answer.

Chapter Three
The Machine

Rick lived in a small, abandoned warehouse in the middle of the forest. He claims that it was the cheapest house option, but Frank knew why Rick really lived there. Lately, Rick's insanely dangerous experiments were so loud that his neighbors began to complain to the police. Especially his nuclear-powered, jet-propelled swivel chair. After that little mess, it took almost seven months for his hair to fully grow back. So, alas, in order to fulfill his life of science and experiments, Rick was forced to isolate himself from the rest of society.

Frank pedaled quickly through the woods. It was the fastest way to get to Rick's warehouse. Plus, he had no pants at the moment, and he certainly didn't want stupid Duncan to give him an eighty dollar fine for partial public nudity.

It was a beautiful day outside, though. Autumn. Frank's favorite time of year. A blanket of brightly colored leaves covered the ground, leaving the trees almost completely bare.

As he rode through the dense forest, things all around him started disappearing again.

VWOOSH! The bush in front of Frank vanished into the air. *VWOOSH!* There went a tree. *VWOOSH!* Another tree.

At that moment, a scary thought went through Frank's mind. *What if my bike disappears while I'm riding it?* He thought. As if on cue, just then, the brake lines on Frank's bicycle vanished. *VWOOSH!*

Frank swerved to the side, now speeding down a steep hill. He pedaled backwards, but it was no use. Before he knew what was going on... WHAM! He zoomed into a tree, and the next thing he knew, he was laying on the ground with a huge gash on his leg.

"Ouch!" Frank yelled. Nobody heard him. His bike lay on the ground beside him, the front tire bent out of shape. *Terrific. Looks like I'm walking...* He thought.

But how could he? With that bad of a gash on his leg, it didn't look like he would be walking anywhere. He was stuck.

But then, the pink bird that kept appearing in Frank's life flew out of a tree and perched itself on his handlebar.

"Why are you stalking me?" Frank said to the bird, firmly. It didn't answer. There was a long, awkward silence.

"I'm talking to a bird," He said to himself. "I must be out of my mind." He looked at the bird, who cocked its head slightly to the side.

"Are *you* the one who's been making everything disappear?" Frank asked the little pink dove, angrily. The bird shook its head.

Frank gasped. This little creature could understand everything Frank was saying.

"Did you just... shake your head?" Frank asked the bird. It nodded.

"So, you *can* understand me?" He asked. The bird nodded once more. Frank was beginning to think he really *was* going insane.

Suddenly, the bird flew off, back into the tree he emerged from before.

"So you're just going to leave me here, then?" Frank hollered at the bird. There was no answer. Frank sighed, and looked down at the ugly looking scrape on his leg.

But then, a moment later, the bird was back. It flew out of the tree and perched itself on Frank's bike handle once again. This time, the bird had a tube of Neosporin and a large band-aid clutched in his beak. It then spat them both out onto the ground beside Frank.

"Hey, thanks!" He said, smiling. "Maybe you're not half bad after all." He applied the Neosporin onto his wound, putting the band-aid on after. "I should name you," He told the bird. The bird tweeted quietly. It was the first time Frank had heard it make a sound. "I'll call you... Reggie. How does that sound?" He asked. The bird tweeted again. "I'll take that as a yes," Frank said.

He stood up, despite the excruciating pain in his left leg.

"What do you know about this rock?" He asked the small bird, curiously. He held up the rock for the bird to see. Reggie eyed the rock for a moment, tweeted loudly, and then flew off once again. Frank figured the bird wanted him to follow it.

"Wait up!" Frank hollered to Reggie as he limped slowly in the bird's direction.

But Reggie flew too fast. Frank couldn't catch up to him. He had no clue which direction he went. Plus, he needed to get to Rick's house. He had no time for chasing birds through the forest.

Luckily, he knew the way back to where his dented, broken bike was lying. He didn't bother trying to drag it with him. It would be useless. So he just left it there and started walking.

As he walked, he admired the scenery and thought about Reggie. What was the story behind that little bird? Did he fly away because he wanted Frank to follow him or was he scared of the rock? The thought mildly alarmed Frank. Maybe this rock really was dangerous…

VWOOSH! Both of Frank's shoes vanished.

"Ugh!" He groaned. His day off wasn't exactly going as planned.

He arrived at Rick's warehouse, trying not to step on anything sharp or prickly with his bare feet. The first thing he noticed was about six large garbage cans with a label on them that read:

CAUTION! NUCLEAR MATERIALS AND SUCH!

Hmmm… Frank thought. *I don't remember those ever being here.* The only aesthetic thing in Rick's front yard was a lone tulip, which had wilted. There was an iron door with a rectangular peephole that opened and closed. It reminded Frank much of a mental institution door.

He banged on the door, shouting, "Hello… Are you home Rick?"

After a moment, the peephole slot slid open, revealing two eerie green eyes.

"Who goes there?" said someone with a heavy British accent.

"It's me, Frank," Frank replied.

"What's the password?" the British man shouted back.

"What? You never had a password!" Frank said.

"I just made one up right now!"

"But if you just made it up then how am I supposed to know what it is?" Frank asked. There was a pause.

"Uh... well, I... alright. Fine. You can come in."

Frank rolled his eyes. Rick was always a little weird.

He entered Rick's humble abode. The first thing he noticed was various test tubes scattered around; some were empty and some were filled with various vibrant colored liquids. On the walls were posters that read *"Eleven out of eleven doctors recommend time travel"*. There were at least a dozen composition notebooks sitting on Rick's desk, probably filled with science stuff and whatnot.

Rick greeted Frank kindly.

"Frank! How pleasant to see you!" He exclaimed. A confused look appeared on his face. "Jumping potatoes! Why aren't you wearing any trousers?"

Frank quickly changed the subject. "Never mind that. A crisis has come up, Rick!" Rick sighed and looked down at the ground.

"Yes, I know. The Braves lost. It's a shame..."

Frank rolled his eyes. "No! Not that. Haven't you noticed everything is disappearing right before our very eyes?" He snapped back.

Rick nodded. "Ah, yes. I've noticed. I've been working on the problem all day and I think I know what's going on."

"You do?" Frank asked, curiously.

"Quite so," Rick replied, pacing the room while he talked. "You see, Albert Einstein once said that all matter in the universe cannot be created nor destroyed. This means that the objects around us aren't vanishing at all. They're simply being teleported to somewhere else. Whoever is responsible must be using some kind of radio signal to make it all disappear. If we could somehow track that signal..."

He was cut off by Frank. "Then we could find out who's causing it all and stop him."

"Precisely! However…" Rick said. "There is another problem. Teleportation technology is decades, maybe even centuries ahead of our time."

Frank was puzzled. "What are you saying?" He asked.

"I'm saying that whoever is causing all of the disappearances must be traveling through time somehow."

Frank just stood there like an idiot with a confused look on his face. It was too much to take in. First everything starts vanishing without warning. Then a weird pink bird starts communicating with him. And now, his insane quantum physicist friend starts rambling on about time travel.

"What?" Frank shouted. "Time travel?"

"Yes. Time travel." Rick replied as he bent over and began typing on his keyboard. "He must have gone into the future, into a period of time in which teleportation is a reality, acquired some sort of teleportation device, then come back to the present and is now making everything vanish."

"But, why?"

"I'm not sure. Maybe it's just a joke."

The TV was blaring in the other room. The anchor on CNN News was talking about the disappearances.

"This just in… The world is in chaos. Cities everywhere are being destroyed due to spontaneous, possibly paranormal disappearances. The foundations of buildings, bridges, even major landmarks are vanishing to unknown locations worldwide. The source of this madness has yet to be discovered. Back to you, Bob…"

Frank looked back at Rick. "We need to get to the bottom of this!" he said.

"But, how?" Rick asked. "We don't know where the source of the teleportation is."

"Come on, Rick! There has to be some way to stop it!" Frank shouted back. He was so frustrated he was raising his voice.

"Well..." Rick said. "Perhaps there is one way..."

Frank's eyes widened. "What is it?" He asked eagerly.

"Never mind. It's too dangerous." Rick replied.

"Tell me what it is!" Frank shouted.

"Well, I'm currently working on a time machine. I was going to suggest traveling into the future and stopping the individual who is causing the vanishings from acquiring the teleportation device in the first place. But I haven't worked out all of the bugs yet. It's way too risky to-"

"We have to! It's our only option!" Frank interrupted.

"No. It's too risky."

"Please?"

"No."

"Please?"

"I said no, Frank."

"You'll probably win the Nobel Prize if we save the world."

"Tempting, but no."

"Come on!"

"Calm down, Frank. I'm sure we'll find another way," said Rick.

VWOOSH! The TV in the other room disappeared. An awkward silence emerged in the room. Frank pulled out the rock from his pocket and handed it to Rick.

"What's this?" Rick asked.

"It's a rock. A wizard gave it to me," Frank replied. A confused look appeared on Rick's face.

"Wait... what?" He asked.

"It's a long story," Frank replied. And so, Frank told Rick about everything that had happened to him so far. The wizard. Reggie. Everything else. After he was finished explaining, Rick didn't seem confused at all. He just sat there, emotionless.

"You don't believe me, do you?" Frank asked.

Rick stood up. "I don't know. It seems so weird." He said as he studied the rock. "But then again, a lot of weird things have been happening lately."

Frank continued talking. "The strangest thing is: I can't get rid of it. I tried to throw it out the window, but it just came back to me."

"You mean the rock?" asked Rick.

"Yeah," Frank replied. "It's almost as if I'm cursed or something."

For a moment, there was silence as Rick stared down at the rock.

"Follow me," Rick said finally. Frank didn't question as he trailed behind Rick to the basement, just as the table vanished and the computer came crashing to the ground. Rick didn't pay any attention to it. They walked down a long spiral staircase into the pitch black, eerie basement that smelled like dead rats.

"Why are we here?" he asked. Then Rick turned on the lights, which revealed a magnificent, shiny rocket ship that was the size of Frank's house. Frank stood there in amazement, with his mouth wide open.

It was white, but incredibly shiny, with a red stripe on the pointed nose cone.

The basement itself was huge; at least the size of Frank's entire office building. Well... *former* office building. There were toolboxes, piles of scrap metal, and computer parts scattered everywhere.

"Wow…" he whispered to himself.

"This is Amy," Rick said as he pointed to the giant rocket ship.

"Amy?" Frank asked.

"My time machine."

"You named your time machine Amy? You seriously couldn't think of a cooler name?"

"That's not the point! The point is: Amy is going to take us into space and through time."

Frank looked at Rick. "But you said it was too dangerous…" Rick interrupted him.

"Frank, you were right. Look around. The world is disappearing right before our eyes. Who will stop it if we don't?" Frank knew that Rick had a good point, but he was still skeptical.

"Are you sure it's safe?" He asked, looking up at Amy. The thing was enormous. It looked like something that would belong to NASA.

"Who cares about safety at this point?" Rick asked. "If we go, we might die. But if we don't go, we also might die. We have nothing to lose."

Frank considered his options for a long time before he finally agreed.

"Okay," He said simply.

"Excellent! I'll get her engine started," Rick exclaimed as he began to dig through one of his various toolboxes. Meanwhile, Frank continued to admire the massive rocket ship/time machine that was Amy.

"What fuels it anyway?" Frank asked.

"Her," Rick corrected without looking up.

25

"Fine. Her," Frank said, rolling his eyes. Rick started explaining.

"I have concocted the perfect combination of uranium and Lysol™ Disinfectant spray to fuel Amy's time circuits. I call it: TimeJuice! I have supplied us enough TimeJuice to take us to the future and back. But be cautious; direct exposure to the uranium may result in skin cancer. Or really bad pimples."

Frank eyed the test tube of bubbling, bright green TimeJuice that sat on the table. "Isn't uranium a highly radioactive element?" he assured Rick.

He watched as Rick picked up a large toolbox and a few liters of TimeJuice. "Yeah, probably," he answered. This only frightened Frank more.

"Hop in," Rick said as he put on a pair of tacky, circular goggles. "But first, you might want to put these on." He tossed another pair to Frank.

"Why do we need these?" Frank asked.

"Oh, you know. Just in the highly unlikely event that something… explodes," Rick replied. Frank didn't question any further and put the goggles on.

They were a bit too tight, but Frank was in no position to complain. So he didn't.

Rick pulled out a remote control from the toolbox. With the press of a button, the roof opened and sunlight poured into the bunker. Amy's white, chrome exterior looked shinier than ever.

"Whoa…" Frank said to himself out loud.

"Pretty cool, eh?" Rick asked. Frank looked back at Rick who was pressing another button on his remote control. This one opened the door to the cockpit, which was suspended ten feet in the air. A ladder descended and Rick began to climb to the top.

"Come on, now!" Rick shouted to Frank, who was still admiring Amy. He trailed behind Rick, who was already in the cockpit, pouring TimeJuice into the main fuel supply.

The cockpit itself was fairly small. There were only two seats, a window, a control panel, and a fire extinguisher that was mounted to the wall.

Frank sat down and strapped himself in. Rick did the same.

"You do know how to fly this thing, right?" Frank asked Rick with a worried expression on his face.

"Of course. She's voice activated. Watch this," Rick replied as he cleared his throat. "Amy, awaken!" He shouted. Amy's systems started immediately. All the lights in the cockpit flickered to life at once. A computerized female voice began to speak.

"Systems: ON. Good afternoon, Rick," She said. Rick gave Amy more commands.

"Amy, engine start," He said to her.

"ENGINE: STARTING…" She replied. The engine started promptly.

"Activate thrusters."

"THRUSTERS ACTIVATED."

Rick looked at Frank. "Are you ready?" He asked.

"Ready as I'll ever be," Frank replied. He still had doubts, but Rick was right. There was nothing to lose.

"Alrighty then," Rick confirmed. "Amy… Blast off!"

"BLASTING OFF. HAVE A NICE FLIGHT, RICK," said Amy. Frank looked out the small window and saw smoke filling the entire bunker. After a few seconds, Amy was rising into the air. Frank was still nervous about his upcoming journey into the future. But in the meantime, he decided to sit back, relax, and enjoy the magnificent view of the forest as he rocketed into the stratosphere.

Chapter Four
The Journey

A mixed feeling of motion sickness and amazement filled Frank's body at once. He stared out the window, admiring the clouds as the rocket shot into the sky.

"Is this your first time flying?" Rick asked, interrupting Frank's thoughts.

"No," Frank replied. "I've flown before." He hardly ever traveled, but he had, in fact, flown in various planes before. But never in a rocket ship; much less a time machine. However, in the few occasions he did fly in a plane, it wasn't a very pleasant experience.

He'd usually book his flight at the last minute and get the crummiest seat on the plane. His seat was always in the very back, where it smelled like expired Sour Patch Kids™. There'd be a window, but the loud turbine was always blocking his view. Plus, the back of the plane is where the flight attendants sit. And they are always talkative and annoying. Aside from the delicious peanuts, flying for Frank was never fun.

But still, despite all that, he was partaking in the miracle of human flight. And this time, it was in a rocket ship time machine! Frank felt amazing.

"We're entering space!" Rick exclaimed. This made Frank want to look out the window even more. What he saw was absolutely incredible.

The deep void of outer space was as dark as the night. The earth looked as though it was a giant, glowing blue sphere of life. Frank never thought space was as peaceful as it really was. His day off truly was going better than he expected.

His thoughts were interrupted by Rick. "Hold on to something," he commanded.

"Why?" Frank questioned as his attention turned from the window to Rick.

"You see, the way time travel works is based around the fact that the faster you're traveling, the more time speeds up for everyone else. Therefore, we're going to be orbiting the earth at nearly the speed of light."

"What!?" Frank hollered.

"Relax, Frank," Rick assured. "It's perfectly safe… probably. And the best part is: it'll only feel like ten minutes to us, but over a hundred years to the rest of the world!"

"But, how will we get back?" asked Frank.

"Simple," Rick replied. "All we have to do is travel in the opposite direction at the same speed, thus contrasting with the earth's orbit, which will no doubt send us back in time!"

Frank wasn't so convinced. "Are you certain it will work?"

"Of course," Rick continued. "It may not be a hundred percent accurate, but we'll land right back in the present, give or take a few years."

"Well… okay. I mean… you *are* the quantum physicist," Frank said. Rick grinned.

"Excellent!" He exclaimed. "Strap in," He concluded simply.

The way to strap into the seats was similar to the way you would strap yourself into a rollercoaster seat. There was a large metal bar that came down and fastened you in. There were also handlebars suspended from the ceiling.

"Put this on," said Rick, handing Frank an astronaut helmet.

"What's it for?" Frank asked.

"You need it so that the G Force doesn't make your brain implode inside your skull," Rick replied as if it hardly mattered. Frank gulped loudly. His trembling hands took the helmet and he put it on.

"Amy!" Rick commanded. His voice was muffled due to his helmet. "Activate hyper speed turbines!"

"HYPER SPEED TURBINES ACTIVATING," Amy's computerized voice hollered throughout the cockpit.

Suddenly, she zoomed forward at nearly light-speed without any acceleration at all. The many various stars now looked like lines. Frank felt so sick to his stomach that he blacked out.

Frank awakened to the view of space once more. He still had his helmet on, but Rick didn't. So he assumed it was safe to take it off. Rick was typing away on a laptop that was installed into the main control panel. He looked over at Frank.

"Ah… finally awake, I see," he said. Frank still had a massive headache and didn't respond right away.

"Um… yeah. What'd I miss?" he asked.

"Welcome to the year 2117!" Rick exclaimed, beaming with glee. Frank was amazed.

"Awesome!" He said to Rick. He couldn't help but look out the window once more. But as he did, he noticed that the earth looked a lot darker. A lot… smoggier.

He also caught a glimpse of the moon, which was now covered with all sorts of space equipment and such. There appeared to be a moon base that NASA had set up. "Interesting…" He said to himself. Rick overheard.

"What's interesting?" Rick asked. Frank was so preoccupied with the window that he almost forgot that Rick was with him.

"Look at the moon," He replied. Rick peered out the window.

"Hmm… That is rather peculiar. I don't see why humans would be interested in the moon again. We've seen all we need to see. It's just… rocks," said Rick. Frank smiled.

"Maybe we found *aliens!*" Frank added, jokingly. Rick just rolled his eyes. Frank changed the subject.

"What time of year is it on earth?" He asked.

"Well I'm not certain, but looking at the tilt of the earth's axis, I'd say that it's about springtime. Month 5 or Month 6 perhaps."

That was another weird thing that Rick did. Instead of saying May or June, he'd say Month 5 and Month 6. For some odd reason, it really annoyed Frank.

Rick pressed some more buttons on his laptop and the control panel.

"We should be landing soon. I've marked the landing zone. You may want to hold on to something as we re-enter the atmosphere," he said. Frank strapped in, put on the tight goggles, and held on to the handle above him.

"Amy, prepare for landing," Rick commanded.

"RE-ENTRY WILL COMMENCE IN T MINUS 20 SECONDS," she replied. Rick turned to Frank

"Oh, and one more thing," Rick added. "Put on some pants when we get to the future." Frank had completely forgotten that that his pants had disappeared earlier.

"Got it," He said.

Then Amy began to accelerate automatically.

"RE-ENTRY COMMENCING." Downward she sped, hurdling towards the earth. Rick was tugging on a joystick that controlled Amy manually. Frank held the handle above him, even though it probably wasn't necessary. Within a minute, the ground came into view. They were going incredibly fast. Frank braced himself for the worst while Rick pulled up on the joystick. Then…

THUD… Amy slammed into the earth. Every bone in Frank's body jolted to life. She skidded through the land before slowly coming to a complete stop.

There was a pause.

"ARRIVAL TIME: MAY 21, 2117. HAVE A NICE DAY, RICK," she said; her computerized voice breaking the silence. "AND WELCOME TO THE FUTURE.

Chapter Five
The Ruins

Rick opened the hatch and light flooded into the ship. Frank stared out into the world. What used to be a forest was now a field of dead grass, shrubs, and tree stumps, the grey sky overhead. They both stepped out of Amy and observed the future.

"It's different from what I expected," said Rick.

"Yeah. It's much more… bleak," Frank agreed. They both continued to look around.

"Amy isn't in that bad of shape," Rick said, looking at Amy. "Sure, she's stuck into the ground, but at least she's not broken." It was a good thing, too. If Amy were to stop working, they would have no way of making it back home. Rick tossed Frank a pair of jeans from the cockpit of Amy. He quickly put them on; they were a size large, but it was hardly noticeable.

"Where's the rest of civilization?" Frank asked.

"Excellent question. I haven't the slightest idea," Rick replied.

Suddenly, Frank heard a 'tweet' in the distance. It was faint, but still audible.

"Did you hear that?" He asked.

"Hear what?" asked Rick, looking at Frank. He heard another 'tweet'.

"That! Did you hear that?" He asked once again. Before Rick had time to answer, Reggie popped out of a shrub.

"It's Reggie!" Frank hollered in excitement. He ran to the little, pink bird. He extended his arm for Reggie to sit on.

"That's Reggie? Well, what's he doing in the future?" Rick yelled at Frank from a distance.

"I don't know," Frank said. "Reggie, do you know how to get back to civilization?" He asked the bird. Reggie tweeted once more and flew off to the east. "Come on, Rick. We need to follow him!"

Rick didn't feel entirely comfortable following a strange pink bird he had never seen before, but what other choice did he have? So he began walking right behind Frank. Reggie fluttered along; Frank and Rick trailing behind.

Reggie soared through the grey, smoggy air for about five minutes before finally stopping at what looked like an abandoned town.

"Are we here?" asked Frank. Reggie gazed at him and nodded quickly. Frank and Rick scanned the area. There were about seven or eight houses. If you could even classify them as houses; they were more like makeshift houses or shacks. Frank and Rick both sensed an eerie presence. There was nobody around, which only added to the creepiness. The place was a ghost town.

"What is this place?" Rick asked to nobody in particular. He was hoping that Reggie could provide some sort of answer, but he was nowhere in sight. He flew away silently.

"Reggie? Where'd you go?" Frank hollered. Just then, they heard a door slam. In the distance, obscured by the smog, a figure stood. Frank and Rick just looked at each other. The figure moved closer and closer, until it came into view.

It was a boy. He looked to be about sixteen or so. He had shaggy, brown hair, was wearing jeans and a jacket, although they looked ratty and torn, and he also had a gas mask on. He slowly removed the gas mask, revealing his face. As he looked at Frank and Rick he started to speak.

"It's quite dangerous to be outside with the smog this bad. Why don't you come inside?" He said.

"Um… okay," Rick said. Without any further questioning, they both followed the boy inside of the largest of the eight houses.

The house was made entirely out of wood and looked to be just less than two-hundred square feet. Inside, there was a kettle, a wooden chair that looked like it was uncomfortable, a table that had a stack of books on it, and a map that was taped to the wall with red thumb tacks pinned on certain locations.

"My name's Ashton. Ashton Castles," the boy said. He began to pour water from the kettle into three glasses.

Castles. Interesting… Frank thought

"I'm Frank. And this is Rick," Frank replied. Rick waved slightly.

"Nice to meet you," Ashton greeted with a light smile. Frank and Rick smiled back. There was a small silence as Ashton continued to pour the water into the glasses. Then Ashton continued to talk.

"The smog's been almost unbearable since The Invasion, eh?" He said. Frank and Rick nodded in agreement, although they were completely unsure of what he was talking about. Ashton picked up his glass and took a sip.

"So, what brings you to The Hollows?" He asked. There was an awkward silence

"Well… we're from the year 2013." Frank said.

Ashton looked up from his glass. "You're serious?" He asked. "So are you like… time travelers?"

"Yes," Rick answered. "Our time machine crash landed about a five minutes' walk from here." Ashton just sat there.

"You don't believe us, do you?" Frank asked as he gazed down at the floor.

"No. I completely believe you. I heard the crash," Ashton said as he continued to sip from his glass. "2013; a lot of things happened in 2013."

"We know," said Rick. "Everything started to disappear into thin air. I figured that whoever was making it all vanish was using some sort of teleportation technology. So we traveled to this year to see if that technology existed yet so we could stop that person from getting their hands on it."

"Well…" Ashton said. "Good plan, but it's too late. Cities everywhere have been destroyed because of the disappearances. It's why we live in isolation from society."

"But how is that possible?" Frank asked. Rick buried his head into his hands.

"Ugh!" He yelled. "How could I have been so stupid?" Frank and Ashton stared at Rick and his frustration.

"What's wrong?" Frank asked. Rick looked up.

"You see, when we went into the future, we arrived in the alternate future. The future in which the disappearances have already taken place," He said. "We traveled to the wrong future!"

There was a silence. Then Ashton began to speak.

"I think it's time I enlighten you on what's happened since you left," He said, his quiet voice filling the silent air. Frank and Rick just nodded and sat down.

"It all started in 2013. Everything in the world began to vanish. There was no warning, or prediction of what was going to disappear next. Everything from buildings to pen caps just... vanished sporadically. NASA tried to track the signal of the teleportation, but it was no use. They found nothing. Before long, civilizations were collapsing.

"Then, in 2014, just a year later, terrifying machines began to rise from the ground. They were ten feet tall, and had beams that made anything or anyone in their path vanish. Military forces attacked the machines, but to no avail. When one went down, ten more sprouted up, each one producing massive amounts of smog into the air.

"By the second half of the twenty-first century, NASA re-initiated the moon program and made moon bases, hoping that the moon would be a safe haven from the attacks of the machines.

"Those who stayed on the earth either live underground, or in isolation, much like me." Ashton was finished talking, and Frank and Rick just sat there, taking in all of this information. There was a pause. Then Ashton spoke again.

"That's pretty much everything. Millions have already disappeared to an unknown location. The machines stalk the land."

"Well, then how do we stop them?" Frank asked.

"There's only one way we can stop them," said Rick. "We need to travel back to the present and finish this before it starts." He looked at Ashton. "We need to get back to Amy," he said.

"Who's Amy?" Ashton asked with a puzzled look on his face.

"My time machine," said Rick. Ashton chuckled.

"You named your time machine Amy?" He asked, laughingly. Frank chuckled as well. Rick just sighed and rolled his eyes.

"You might need these," Ashton said. He held two gas masks. Frank took them.

"Thanks," said Frank. He smiled. Ashton smiled back. The gas masks were tightly fitting around Frank's head.

"Thanks for the help, Ashton," said Rick as he opened the door that lead to the grim, dreary outside land.

"No problem," said Ashton. Frank and Rick stepped quietly into the smog.

They dashed through what once was a forest. They made their way to Amy who was still embedded into the earth, hardly damaged.

"Amy!" Rick hollered. "Systems activate! We need to go back to the past!" All of Amy's lights flashed on, glowing bright crimson. Her computerized voice was eerier than ever.

"I'M SORRY, RICK. I'M AFRAID I CAN'T LET YOU DO THAT."

Chapter Six

The Escape

Amy's systems roared to life at once. She began to shake and twitch out of control. Slowly she shifted and changed. Within fifteen seconds, she had morphed into a fifteen foot robot with stereotypical glowing red eyes. She growled a terrifying robotic, mechanical hiss, and punched the ground, leaving a crater the size of a piano.

Frank and Rick, as you might have guessed, simultaneously screamed like little schoolgirls and darted into the forest, flailing their arms. Amy stomped behind; each step shook the ground as if an earthquake was taking place. Frank and Rick scurried about, in panic, like mice being chased by a ferocious cat.

"What's happening?" Frank shouted as he sprinted.

"Amy's artificial intelligence chip must have somehow become corrupted. She now wants to kill us for whatever reason!" Rick yelled back. Amy's giant iron fist slammed into the earth again, tearing through the ground, horrifically.

"That's ridiculous!" Frank hollered.

"Well, it's happening," yelled Rick. Amy persisted. She continued to chase them through the forest, tossing trees aside.

Suddenly two machines popped out. They were ten feet tall, just like Ashton described them. They were still smaller than Amy, but equally as frightening. Now three giant, monstrous robots were hunting down Frank and Rick.

Just then, purple laser beams emitted from the machines' hands, similar to the way webs shoot out of Spiderman's hand. Everything in the lasers' path disappeared.

All Frank and Rick could do was dodge the lasers to the best of their ability.

Before long, they approached a pond. They seemed to have outrun the machines, but they had nowhere to go. Swimming away would only make them an easier target. Plus, the water looked extremely filthy.

But then, all of a sudden, they appeared, roaring with rage. The two machines raised their arms, preparing to fire another beam. Then…

Vroooooom! CRASH! A brown, rusty truck came out of nowhere and slammed into the machines, knocking them down. Their systems slowly shut off. The tinted window of the truck rolled down, and Ashton's face was revealed.

"Hop in," he said. They did.

Amy emerged from the distance, dashing towards them, getting closer.

"Drive!" Frank shouted. Ashton stepped on the gas just as Amy lunged forward. They sped away at the last second and Amy tumbled into the water.

Sparks flew. She shorted out and sank into the depths of the pond.

Amy… had been terminated.

Chapter Seven
The Recollection

Ashton sped along until they reached an abandoned highway. Frank and Rick's hearts raced at a million beats per minute. For a minute or so, nobody talked. Then Ashton spoke up.

"I... uh... heard the noises. I came to see what was happening," he said as he continued to drive.

"Thank you for saving us," Frank said with a smile. Ashton smiled as well.

"No problem," he replied. "Anything to save the world."

"But without Amy, we have no way of making it back to the past," mentioned Rick. Everyone was silent for a brief moment as they examined their options. Then, Frank's face lit up, for he had an idea.

"We could use the spare parts from the machines that Ashton ran over," Frank suggested.

"Perhaps... perhaps..." Rick said as he rubbed his chin in a thoughtful manner. "But it'll take more than just a couple of machines to reconstruct a time machine, especially one as massive as Amy."

Frank spoke again. "That's why we'll have to kill more of them."

"What? We almost died!" Rick exclaimed, almost shouting.

"We have to try," said Frank.

"Well, what about the TimeJuice?" asked Rick. "I can't just get uranium at the local convenience store. Even in the future." Frank completely forgot about the TimeJuice.

"You're right. We lost it all when Amy jumped into the pond…" he said, sighing. Ashton entered the conversation.

"Maybe not," he said. Frank and Rick were both lost. "I know of an old marina. It's abandoned now, but they have scuba diving suits there. Maybe we could retrieve it… assuming it hasn't spilled into the water."

Rick chimed in. "That's not a bad idea. I put the TimeJuice in a Plexiglas container. I doubt it has shattered, even after Amy turned into a vicious robot."

Frank thought about the idea. It seemed so far-fetched. But it was their only hope. The only other option was to stay in the future and eventually die from the machines. And that wasn't exactly on Frank's to-do list.

"Okay. It sounds like a plan," he said. "We need to get parts though. Ashton and I will kill more machines. Rick can use the parts to reconstruct the time machine. Then, we'll scuba dive down and get the TimeJuice. This might actually work."

"It has to work," Rick added.

Ashton and Frank dropped Rick back off at The Hollows. With the two dead machines by the pond, he had everything he needed to at least get started on a basic design.

And so, they took off in Ashton's rusty truck, into the woods.

For a while, nobody said anything. Ashton just drove on into what seemed to be and endless forest. Finally, Frank boldly broke the eerie silence.

"So what exactly is 'the Hollows'?" He asked.

"It's our little community. It's nothing special, really. There used to be dozens of people in the Hollows… Now there's just me," Ashton replied, eyes locked on the road.

"So… uh… how long have you lived in The Hollows?" he asked.

"Quite a while," Ashton responded. "There used to be a whole community there. That's why there are so many houses. But over time, everyone died of either diseases or disappeared by the machines. After that, it was just me and my father. And ever since he went into these very woods two years ago and never returned, it's just been me, living by myself."

"Oh," Frank said. He felt bad for asking about the subject. It seemed like it was a part of Ashton's past that he didn't want to bring up, like a time capsule that's not quite ready to be opened. So he dropped the subject.

Within a moment, they reached the same highway they were earlier. And right away, they noticed a machine wandering in the distance. Ashton floored it.

Within five seconds, he had accelerated to eighty-eight miles an hour. If only traveling back in time was that simple… Frank was actually surprised at how fast the clunky truck could travel. Then again, he had no idea how much technology had progressed in a hundred and four years. Then…

KASLAM! Ashton collided with the machine. It tried to fire its beam of bright violet at them in time, but it was far too late.

Its head smashed into the windshield, denting the roof with its metallic cranium.

"Ugh!" Ashton exclaimed. "It was in good condition!" To Frank, it seemed like that would be the least of Ashton's worries. THUD. The machine and the ground made forceful contact. Its systems powered down, and Ashton and Frank both got out of the truck to retrieve it.

It was certainly heavy, however it was a little lighter than Frank thought it would be. He wondered if Rick was having a hard time recovering the two dead machines by the pond.

They hauled the machine into the back of the pickup and drove along.

Frank was relieved. If it was this easy to destroy the machines, then they would have enough parts to recreate the machine in no time. Within the next two hours, they had successfully totaled three machines and tossed them in the back of the truck.

In that time, Frank noticed that the license plate had expired in 2055. Over sixty years ago. Frank was shocked. If the license plate was that expired, then they must've lived in isolation for an incredibly long time. It also meant that the truck was extremely old. So Frank assumed that automobiles had become more technologically advanced over the years if the truck was at least sixty-two years old. *Interesting…* Frank thought to himself.

The truck was moving much slower now. Not only that, but it was also making really weird sounds.

"It seems like the weight of the machines is straining my engine," Ashton sighed. "We should be able to make it to the marina, though." That was a good thing. Frank had done enough walking in one week (or technically, one hundred and four years).

Before long, they were there, at the abandoned marina. *It seems like pretty much everything in this Godforsaken future is abandoned.* Frank thought. There were about six different docks, each with about twelve boats. They looked new and high tech, like some that would be invented in the future. But they were old and covered in mildew and rust, which only made them look like an eye sore.

There was a long dock that led to a small shack, just sitting there at the end of the dock. As they got closer, Frank noticed a faded sign that read: Welcome to Pleasant Shores! However the 'H' was missing, so it read: Welcome to Pleasant Sores! *That's odd... Frank thought. Most sores I've gotten weren't exactly pleasant. Clever wordplay I suppose.*

Ashton approached the door, which was littered with cobwebs. He hesitated, as if he was afraid that a skunk or something was going to pop out of the shack that probably hadn't been opened in years.

He opened the door ever so slowly and peeked in to see what was inside. The shack was a shop. The florescent lights on the ceiling automatically turned on. There were all sorts of aquatic accessories on the walls. Everything from surf boards to tube calk, whatever that was. But, sure enough there was some sort of creature inside. At least five of them.

They were insanely creepy. They had bright green eyes, their pupils taking up ninety percent of their eye. They also were about a foot and a half long and had six sets of teeth, three on the top and three on the bottom. Frank noticed that they also had sharp needles sticking out of their back and it seemed like they were drooling blue slime.

Frank was startled and jolted backwards.

"Just don't move," Ashton said, almost in a whisper. "They're stupid. They can't see you if you don't move. Just like T-Rex's."

"What are they?" Frank asked, his heart still racing.

"Smeekrats," responded Ashton. "They're a crossbreed of moles and porcupines. Over the years they evolved, adapting to the constant smog."

Moles and porcupines... thought Frank. *Quite an odd combination.*

And so, they inched ahead slowly. The smeekrats didn't seem to notice them. Frank noticed they were making weird, quiet gargling noises, as if they were choking on slime.

"I think we're safe," Ashton whispered.

"Are you sure?" asked Frank.

"Probably," Ashton assured, although there was a bit more uncertainty in his voice than his words suggested.

"On three," he said. "One... two..." Frank prepared to sprint to the back of the shop.

"Three!" Ashton yelled. "Go! Go!" Frank ran. The smeekrats hissed a menacing hiss and chased them both across the shop. They were incredibly quick. Frank and Ashton continued to dash through the shop as several smeekrats popped out of nowhere. Frank could feel the adrenaline pumping through his body.

Suddenly, one lunged forward and chomped at Ashton's leg.

"Ow!" he yelped in pain. But he continued to run forward. Eventually, they reached a high shelf.

"We have to climb it!" shouted Frank. He glanced down at Ashton's leg. There was a deep bite mark that was covered in dark blue sludge. It didn't seem like Ashton would be able to climb anything, but he persevered and jumped up, grasping the side of the shelf.

Frank had reached the top and desperately tried to help Ashton, who was struggling to get up. As Frank looked down at the floor, his jaw dropped. There was a sea of about four dozen disgusting smeekrats, all of which were trying to kill Ashton and Frank. Once Ashton finally got up to the top, they were already surrounded by fifty of the little buggers, twelve feet in the air. They were stuck.

"What now?" Ashton asked.

"I'm not sure," Frank replied. The smeekrats began climbing up the side of the shelf with their slimy legs. He scanned the area to see if there was anything they could use to fend them off. Even if it was only temporary. So he reached underneath to see what was hanging on the shelf. The only thing in reach was a pink, flowery boogie board. *It'll work.* Frank thought.

One came up and jumped into the air, prepared to pounce on Frank.

WHAM! He batted the thing to the floor, just in time for three more to arrive. With his good leg, Ashton punted one of them off the edge. One by one they battled the smeekrats as they swarmed the shelf. There seemed to be no end to the madness. They were multiplying by the minute. There were now about a hundred of them crawling about.

Then the shelf collapsed. Rubble and dust filled the air as the shelf came crashing down.

"Jump!" Ashton shouted at the last minute. Frank didn't see how Ashton could jump with his hurt leg, but he did. And Frank did too.

They grabbed hold of the lights hanging from the ceiling. The shelf fell right on top of the army of smeekrats, obliterating them all. All was silent.

"Well that was close," Frank said. It was an understatement.

"Yeah, it was," Ashton replied. "My leg feels numb."

"Does that usually happen when you get bitten by a smeekrat?" Frank asked.

"I've heard it does, but I've never been bitten before," Ashton responded. Frank looked down at Ashton's wound again. The dark blue sludge was still there, covering the painful looking bite. His leg now looked paler than the other leg.

"How do we get down?" Ashton asked. Frank looked around for a way to get back down safely.

"We could jump down to that other shelf," Frank suggested. Ashton agreed and hopped down to the shelf adjacent to the light. Frank followed.

They climbed down and were greeted by smeekrat corpses. Hundreds of them. The floor was coated blue because of all the smeekrat slime. Ashton began to search for the scuba suits, remembering to be cautious just in case there were any smeekrats poking around. Frank just stood there.

"I found them!" Ashton hollered from the very back of the shop. There they were. Exactly two of them left. Complete with a helmet, air tank, even flippers.

"Let's suit up," said Frank. He went to one of the back rooms and Ashton stayed in the shop area to get suited.

Frank put on the jumpsuit and screwed in the helmet. He was ready. He walked out, feeling ready to recover the TimeJuice that was sitting at the bottom of the pond. Ashton was already suited up as well.

"Are we ready?" he asked.

"We're ready," Frank replied. Ashton tossed him an under-water flashlight.

"Let's go then," said Ashton. They walked past the massive puddle of smeekrat sludge and outside. They hopped in the truck and drove away, dressed in their diving attire.

Luckily, there weren't any more machines in the way of their path. Ashton's truck could hardly take any more damage, and it would be impossible to avoid one if it were to see them.

They arrived a few minutes later to the exact spot where Amy tumbled into the pond. Frank remembered the area far too well. They got out of the truck and prepared to plunge into the water. It looked even filthier than last time.

"Let's go," Ashton said. He then proceeded to dive in. Frank followed, jumping into the dark depths of the pond.

Chapter Eight

The Plunge

At first, he saw nothing but blackness. There was a huge drop off; no shelf of any kind; it was almost as if they were swimming over a cliff that was submerged in water. There didn't seem to be any sea life. If there was, Frank couldn't see it.

Just then, Frank noticed a beam of light up ahead in the distance. It was probably Ashton turning on his flashlight.

"Can you hear me?" a voice said, startling Frank. It was Ashton, talking to him through a microphone in the helmet.

"Yeah, I can hear you," he responded.

"Great," said Ashton, his voice was slightly distorted. "You may want to turn on your flashlight now." Frank turned it on; the light revealed dozens of tiny minnows that were mindlessly swimming around, but nothing more than that.

"Here she is," Ashton said through the microphone. Sure enough, Amy came into view. She was almost completely destroyed and covered in algae. The sight reminded Frank of a sunken battleship.

"Let's search for the TimeJuice," Frank suggested. They began to look around. Frank felt there was something eerie about Amy's presence. Almost as if he was worried Amy would come back to life and try to kill them again. The idea was preposterous, but it still gave him the chills. Frank tried to forget about it and continued to look for the TimeJuice.

They searched for five full minutes and found nothing.

"Do you see it yet?" Frank asked.

"No. Nothing yet," replied Ashton.

But then, Frank saw it. The shimmering vial of bright green TimeJuice. It was as good as new! A pang of happiness and relief shot through Frank.

"I found it!" he exclaimed.

"Excellent! I'll meet you up top," Ashton replied. Then he swam upwards.

Frank went to retrieve the TimeJuice, which was slightly embedded into the sea floor. He picked up the bottle and began to follow Ashton, but something in the corner of his eye caught his attention. It was... shiny, like a gem or something. He swam towards it, and realized that it was a beautiful neon pink crystal just sitting there a few meters away from Amy. *What the heck?* Frank thought. He picked it up and swam to the shore.

Ashton was waiting for him when he emerged from the pond. He had already started the truck.

"What's that?" He asked pointing down at the pink crystal.

"I'm not sure," Frank said. "I found it at the bottom of the pond." He handed it to Ashton who began to examine it.

"It looks familiar..." Ashton said. "I think I've seen this before."

"What?" asked Frank. "You have?"

"Yeah. What do you think it means?" He asked Frank, handing the rock back to him.

"I'm not sure, but I think we should keep it. Just in case," Frank replied. Ashton agreed and placed the crystal in the pocket of his dry pants.

"I'm going to get changed out of this suit," Ashton said.

"Me too," said Frank. They changed into their dry clothes, got into the truck, and headed back to the Hollows.

Chapter Nine

The Counterstrike

The entire ride back to the Hollows Frank was thinking about the crystal. *What does it mean?* He thought. *Maybe Rick used it as a power source for Amy or something?* He wasn't sure. Maybe it had no significance. All he knew was that they had the TimeJuice. That was all that mattered for now.

They approached the Hollows to find Rick still working on the new time machine. There was a large metal cylinder that was about twenty feet in diameter on the ground. It looked like some sort of basic base for the new time machine.

They stepped out of the truck and were greeted by Rick, who was clutching a wrench.

"Greetings! How goes it? Did you bring back parts?" He asked.

"Yep. They're in the back of the truck there," Frank responded. He pointed at the mountain of scrap metal that once was a pack of deadly machines.

"Excellent!" Rick exclaimed, walking towards the truck. "It won't be long before we're back to the past!" Frank could hardly wait. He was sick of the deadly, gloomy, smoggy future.

"But don't forget," Frank reminded Rick. "We still have to make things right in the past and defeat whoever is responsible for all of this madness." Rick hadn't forgotten. He was ready. Hoping for the best. Expecting the worst.

For some reason, Frank remembered at that moment what the wizard guy had said to him earlier. 'Use the rock to defeat the antagonist'. Whoever it was that was causing the disappearances must be the antagonist he was referring to. But if that was the case, how did he know? It was another mystery that left Frank puzzled.

Rick began to take the parts out of the truck and set them on the ground right next to his cylinder. Ashton started to help.

All of a sudden, they heard a distorted groaning noise in the distance.

"Did you hear that?" Frank asked. Before anyone had time to answer, about eight machines burst from the trees. They were everywhere; purple beams flew through the air. Frank had no choice but to hide under the truck.

There was chaos for a minute. Frank had no idea as to where Rick or Ashton was. He hoped they had escaped somehow. All Frank could do at the moment was hide, which frustrated him. Then, the truck vanished. *Oh no...* Frank thought as he made a run for the woods. Everything was gone. The houses. The truck. Rick's metal cylinder. It had all disappeared. There was nothing left.

Frank was still running as the machines blasted their endless volley of beams at them. There was no use. There were too many of them. Frank tripped and plummeted to the ground. Then…

VWOOSH!

Frank had vanished.

At first, he felt nothingness. Frank was just floating in an abyss of null, unable to feel, see, and hear anything. There was only… nothing. But he was still alive. He could *think*.

Suddenly, he was lying on the ground, surrounded by an infinite whiteness. Everywhere was pure white; it seemed like he was standing on an invisible floor inside a cloud. All was silent.

Frank stood up and looked around. He could see clearly, although there was no light source anywhere in sight.

"Hello?" He yelled. There was no echo, or response. Just whiteness.

"Hello!?" He repeated, louder this time, only to get the same result.

All of a sudden, the scenery changed. The white void slowly began to morph into a stone wall. Then two, then three. Soon, Frank was enclosed in a large room made out of stone. The room was about twenty-five square meters and the ceiling was about seven meters high.

Then, the floor began to change into stone as well. Pretty soon, he was standing inside what seemed to be a giant castle room. There was a hooded figure standing on the other side of the room. An eerie silhouette in the distance. He was twitching uncontrollably.

"At long last," a raspy voice spoke. "We meet. Frank… Smith…"

"He… hello there," Frank stuttered. The figure continued to twitch. "Are you okay?" The figure turned its head one hundred and eighty degrees, like an owl. His face was completely black under his hood, and two glowing red eyes were revealed.

"For the first time in a hundred and four years, I'm fine."

Chapter Ten

The Endgame

Frank just stood there, trying to comprehend what the figure was trying to say. Where was he? Why was he there? Who was the mysterious figure on the other side of the room? He had so many questions.

"Who are you? Why am I here?" He asked the figure, who had stopped twitching.

"All your questions will be answered soon enough, Frank," his scary, raspy voice said. "Allow me to explain to you what is happening." He slowly walked towards Frank, and it became clear that he was faceless. He was dressed in a hooded black cloak, and clutched a remote control to something in his long, thin, blue fingers.

"As you may have already guessed, I am the one who has been causing all of the mysterious disappearing objects. Surprise! The cat is out of the bag," he admitted without any trace of remorse. "What an odd earthling expression... the cat's out of the bag. What was the cat doing in the bag in the first place?"

"You!" Frank hollered as he attempted to charge at the hooded figure. But he couldn't. He was stuck… as if his feet were super glued to the floor beneath him. *What the…?* He thought to himself.

"Don't even bother trying to attack me mortal; it's impossible. I am way over here, and you're stuck right there.

"Anyway, now that that's squared away, I may as well introduce myself. I am Gaylord Bippleblark, high king of Zone G in the universe. Welcome to my secret lair!" Frank began to chuckle.

"What's so funny, mortal?" Gaylord growled. His neon red eyes narrowed, illustrating his anger.

"Gaylord Bricklebark?" Frank asked.

"*Bippleblark!*" Gaylord corrected. "Is there a problem with my name?" Frank tried to refrain from laughing, but he couldn't. "Your parents must've hated you!" he laughed.

"Shut up! I didn't pick it!" Gaylord shouted. Frank continued to giggle. "Enough!" He finally boomed. "Can I finish?"

"Yeah, go ahead," Frank replied. Gaylord cleared his throat.

"As I was saying," Gaylord Bippleblark continued. "There are three minerals that, when combined, can create infinite power; enough to destroy the universe as we know it: the rock of courage, the crystal of wisdom, and the gem of energy. Originally, these three rocks were intended to protect the universe and all that inhabits it. They kept the universe in order. That is until the council of high kings voted to send all three rocks out in different directions deep into space, to protect them from falling into the wrong hands."

"Much like your hands?" Frank cut in.

"Exactly!" Gaylord responded. "And don't interrupt. It's rude, you know." Frank rolled his eyes.

"Where was I? Oh yes! The whole three minerals thing. All three were sent out into the depths of space. I've been trying to find them for a hundred thousand earth years now, but I haven't found anything...until now.

"In the earth year of 2013, I found the gem of energy in the far edge of Zone W."

"So why am I here?" Frank asked.

"I was getting to that, fish face. Let me finish my monologue!" Gaylord snapped.

Fish face? Frank thought.

"Eventually, word got out to the council, and they realized it would only be a matter of time before I found the other two. So they relocated both of them and put them under heavy security. Not just any security... *space* security."

"Sounds spooky," Frank said.

"After years of searching, I realized that the council had put the minerals on the one planet that nobody would bother to look in!"

"You mean Earth?" asked Frank, confused.

"Precisely!" Gaylord exclaimed. "You see, they thought that if someone-I in this case-were to find one of them there, they wouldn't bother to look for the other one in the same place. So they hid them both in plain sight.

"So I used the gem of energy to power a teleportation machine," Gaylord explained as he waved around the remote in his hand. Frank noticed that there was a glowing red, diamond shaped gem connected to the remote, powering it. "That's where you come in. You, Frank, are the missing link to it all. You were chosen to be part of a team to protect the two remaining minerals. I knew that you would try to find the source of the teleportation and put a stop to it. So I lured you into my foolproof trap.

"I created the machines. I corrupted Amy's artificial intelligence chip. I made sure that Amy sank right next to the spot where the crystal of wisdom lay at the bottom of the pond, so that you would find it. I led you to the minerals and waited until they were in your possession. I did everything to make sure that you found the crystal of wisdom. I was behind it all." Gaylord began to laugh maniacally.

"Wait a second," Frank said. "What special team? Who chose me to be a part of this… this special mineral protection squad?"

"Merz," Gaylord replied. "The wizard guy who gave you the rock of courage. He wanted you to keep it safe. He and his stupid little pink bird have been helping you since the beginning of your journey. Little did they know they were only helping you fall into my trap!"

"*His* little pink bird?" Frank asked, confused as could be. "So then why didn't you just use your teleportation doohickey to transport the rocks to your secret lair?"

"Don't you get it?" Gaylord responded. "Merz is a high king of the universe, just like me. He can track the signal of the teleportation device if I teleport them individually. But if *you* have the minerals in your possession, they're your responsibility, which means that he cannot track their locations. He chose you to be a protector. And you failed! Ha!"

"Then why didn't he tell me I was supposed to protect it?" Frank asked in frustration.

"No idea," Gaylord replied, twiddling with his remote control.

"And what about all the stuff you vanished on Earth?" Frank snapped. "Where did all of it go?"

"Don't know. And frankly, I could care less," Gaylord responded, pacing across the room.

"I think you mean you *couldn't* care less," Frank chimed in. Gaylord was puzzled. "What?"

"You said you *could* care less, meaning you do care…" Frank responded.

"Shut it, human! Can I speak for five seconds without you interrupting me?" Gaylord Bippleblark barked. There was a pause. Then Gaylord spoke up once more. "Truthfully, it's all probably in the void of space, gone forever. Unless, of course, you were to hit the restore button on the remote." He waved the remote in front of Frank's face, just out of his reach, taunting him. "But that'll *never* happen!" Gaylord laughed menacingly once again, ran out of breath, coughed, and then continued to laugh menacingly.

"You're evil!" Frank growled. Rage penetrated his body; there was nothing he could do.

"You don't say!" Gaylord answered sarcastically. "That's the point! Now, I'll take those minerals. If you don't mind…"

Frank was reluctant. He didn't want to go down without a fight. But what option did he have? He had failed.

He began to remember the extraordinary journey he had throughout the week. Or technically, century. The machines. The smeekrats. Ashton. And Amy. All of it had amounted to nothing. It was over.

"Today, earthling!" the high king hollered, impatiently.

But just then, as Frank sulked in his misfortune, he noticed something in the corner of the room. A small little flutter in the distance, behind Gaylord. *No. It can't be…* Frank thought to himself. *It is!*

It was Reggie. Reggie! How did he get there? What was he doing in Gaylord's secret lair? Reggie flew above Gaylord's head, unnoticed.

"I'm waiting!" Gaylord shouted. "Fork 'em over!" Frank came up with a plan of action. It was risky, but he had to try; now was his chance.

"Here. You want the rock?" Frank said, voice rising in anger. "Take it!" He took the rock out of his pocket and chucked it as hard as he could at Gaylord's head. *Clunk!*

He hobbled backwards, rubbing his seemingly nonexistent forehead. The remote flew out of his hand and fell onto the floor.

"Ow!" he yelled. "I need ointment for acute pain releif!" He lay on the ground, writhing in pain, giving Reggie just enough time to swoop down and pick up the remote with his beak.

"Hey! What's that blasted bird doing here?" Gaylord hollered. Reggie dropped the remote into Frank's hands. There were only two buttons: *Vanish* and *Restore*. It was as simple as that.

Without a moment of hesitation, Frank pressed the *Restore* button, restoring all that had vanished back to where it belonged.

"No! You didn't hit the *Restore* button, did you?" Gaylord shouted.

Frank aimed the remote directly at him. Without responding, Frank pressed the *Vanish* button. *ZAP!*

A purple beam shot out of the remote, obliterating Gaylord Bippleblark.

"No!" He hollered, his shout echoing as he disappeared from existence. Frank had finally defeated the evil king who was behind all the disappearances.

He finally understood what the wizard, Merz, had meant. *Use the rock to defeat the antagonist.* He eyed the rock of courage, which was now on the ground several feet away. He was a hero. But he didn't feel like one. Was it really that easy? All he did was throw the rock at Gaylord's head. Anyone could've done that.

Reggie sat perched on Frank's shoulder. Like a parrot sitting on the shoulder of a pirate.

He walked over to retrieve the rock, noticing that his feet were no longer stuck to the floor. Reggie fluttered away, hovering over the rock. At the moment he picked it up, Merz appeared, dressed in the exact same wizard robe and wizard hat.

"Congratulations, Frank! You have succeeded!" He exclaimed. Although his smile was obscured by his beard, you could tell it was there.

"Um, thank you... Merz...but what exactly did I succeed in?" Frank replied. "Why did you choose me to a protector?"

"Because, Frank, your life was miserable. You had a terrible job, boss, house; you longed for adventure. I knew that if I put the rock in your hands, you would not only protect the rock, but also try to find the source of the vanishing objects. I didn't tell you because I needed to test you. And you passed with flying colors!" the wizard beamed. "I knew where Gaylord's secret lair was all along. I just needed you to stop him." Reggie flew over to Merz and sat on his head.

"There you are!" the wizard continued, looking at Reggie. "Reggie... that's a nice name." Just then, Rick and Ashton appeared from behind Merz.

"Frank! You're alive!" Rick exclaimed.

"Merz told us everything," this coming from Ashton. "You're the protector!"

"But who was supposed to be the protector for the crystal of wisdom?" Frank asked.

"Stan Castles," Merz replied. Ashton stood there in shock.

"My dad?" Ashton asked.

"His dad?" Frank repeated. Ashton took out the pink crystal from his pocket.

"Precisely. You see, your father decided that he wasn't cut out to be a protector. It was too much responsibility. Too much pressure. So he threw the crystal into the pond.

"Gaylord tried to teleport him to his secret lair in order to obtain the crystal. But he didn't have it. It was sitting at the bottom of the pond." Frank cut in.

"Which is why he needed me to scuba dive down there to retrieve it. It all makes sense now."

Merz turned to Ashton. "Could you be the protector, Ashton?" He asked.

"Me?" Ashton replied.

"Do you think you have what it takes?" asked Merz. Ashton smiled and clutched the crystal.

"I will," he agreed.

"But wait, there's still one more," Frank mentioned, pointing at the gem of energy.

"Ah, yes," the wizard said as he pulled out a slip of paper, seemingly from nowhere. "It appears that Amy Krenshaw of London England is the protector of the gem of energy."

"My sister?" Rick asked.

"His sister?" Frank reiterated. Everyone turned to Rick.

"She's also a scientist. She inspired me to invent a time machine. I named it after her," he enlightened everyone.

"So what do we do next?" Frank asked Merz.

"You need to assemble. You must join forces and never let the rocks fall into the wrong hands," Merz answered.

"So we're going to England, then," Frank concluded.

"We're going to England!" Rick shouted.

"But wait!" Frank said. "What will our lives be like now? I no longer have a job; Ashton's whole future has been changed. What's going to happen now?"

"You can work with me!" Rick suggested. "I could use an assistant." Frank smiled.

"And I'm going with you," said Ashton. "I'm sure the future is a much better place now, but like Merz said, we have to stick together as a team. Together, we'll be unstoppable."

"So let's go!" Rick exclaimed.

Frank's life was different now. His life was no longer a sad miserable abyss. He truly was a hero. And it was time for him to save the world once more.

"Let's go!"

END OF BOOK ONE